THE CARD

Kenny Silva

PublishAmerica
Baltimore

ISBN: 1-60441-320-4
PUBLISHED BY PUBLISHAMERICA, LLLP
www.publishamerica.com
Baltimore

Printed in the United States of America

This book is dedicated to my wife, Cindy, for her unconditional love and support.

Chapter 1

To most thirteen-year-old girls the first week of April is like the first week of any other month. To Dani Rogers, though, it's the greatest time of year. It's not because spring has arrived, and the weather is getting warmer. It's not because school will be out in two months. Her birthday is not until September. No, Dani eagerly awaits for April to arrive because baseball season is finally here! Big deal, you might say? It was for her.

Dani is not the most obvious baseball fan. Looking at Dani does not reveal her secret passion.

She doesn't wear a baseball cap around town or spit out endless statistical dribble about last year's left fielder with the best batting average in night games on Astroturf. Baseball means so much more to her. Baseball is personal.

It became personal because of one person—her grandfather. He introduced her to the sport when she was five. He took her to Shea Stadium to see the Mets and the Dodgers. To this day, she still remembers that first game, clutching a hot dog in one hand and a soda in the other, sitting down the third base line on a day so sun-splashed and bright it was hard not to squint.

"Who's that, Pop?"

"That's the catcher, Dani," her grandfather said.

"Why is he wearing all that stuff?"

"Well, that's his mask and chest protector, and on his legs are his shin guards. All of those protect him from getting hurt."

Dani laughed. "He looks funny. I like him."

From that day on baseball became special to her. The more games she attended, the more she understood. She went from that hot dog clutching five-year-old to someone who could talk to her grandfather about who should hit first in the line-up and when a pitcher should be changed. It was baseball that started the special relationship she had with her grandfather, and it was baseball that was the glue keeping them together.

It wasn't the only thing the two of them talked about, however. Pop always asked how school was going, if she had any boyfriends yet, the funny parts of last week's *Cosby Show* re-run. The two of them were not just grandfather and granddaughter. They were friends.

Dani's attachment to Pop was no accident either. Pop was the man in her life. He gave her the most attention. Dani's father used to be around physically, but he wasn't ever *really* there. If he wasn't at work, he was out with his friends. He spent very little time at home. When he was home the arguments between himself and Dani's mother seemed endless. Dani was torn. She had wished her father was around more, but the more he was, the more her parents fought. She hated that.

With all of the yelling between the two there was no time for Dani's father to give her any attention. The farther apart Dani's parents grew, the closer her and Pop became. Since they only lived three blocks apart at the time, Dani was at her grandparents' house almost every day. Pop saw how Dani needed him, and he was more than happy to be there for her.

Eventually, Dani's parents separated. Although it hurt her inside to see this happen, a part of her was also a little relieved. Maybe mom and dad wouldn't fight so much now, she thought. Maybe while they're separated they can work things out. Dani could only hope.

Her hope, however, faded. After the separation Dani's mom needed to move away—far away. She had a friend that lived in Los Angeles. The company that her friend worked for had some openings. "Maybe you ought to come out and apply for a job, get a fresh start," her friend said. Mrs. Rogers thought long and hard about the idea. Finally, she decided her and Dani did indeed need a new start, just the two of them.

Moving across the country, three thousand miles away, told Dani that her parents would not be getting back together. This was hard. Even though she knew, deep in her heart, that separating was probably for the best, in the back of her mind Dani always wished that her parents might work things out. Being separated not only in their marriage, but now by a great distance, Dani saw a divorce as being the next step.

What hurt Dani as much as this, and maybe even a little more, was moving away from her grandparents. No more baking chocolate chip cookies with grandma, who always let her have a finger-full of the raw dough before they baked them. No more trips to the corner doughnut shop on Sunday mornings. No more card games of "Go Fish", or "War", or "Crazy Eights" on hot summer nights at the kitchen table. No more baseball games with Pop. NO MORE BASEBALL GAMES WITH POP! My gosh, Dani thought. How can this be? What am I going to do?

Dani's moving away hurt Pop, too. He understood why it had to happen, but it still hurt. To ease the loss he had when Dani was gone, he would write to her and call her. To keep their baseball relationship alive he began the tradition of calling every opening day. It was their connection to the past they used to have. Both Dani and Pop respected this tradition as much as their relationship.

Chapter 2

Dani bounced along Market Street with quick, bright steps. As she bounced her dark brown, relaxed hair danced behind her ears and on her shoulders. Usually she strolled home from school with the day's math homework or the next book report on her mind. Today, her thoughts were light. Today, was opening day of the baseball season. Her pace carried her quickly down the sidewalk as her mind wandered, remembering the feelings that past opening days used to bring. Dani's golden brown arms hugged her binder. As she squeezed she pictured her grandfather's face and thought about what new things they might talk about tonight. She knew he would call her. He called every opening day. It was their tradition, a private ritual of their two-person club. As she thought of this she grinned and hugged that binder just a little bit tighter.

He usually called about seven o'clock. He lived in Brooklyn, New York, which is three hours later than Dani's home in Los Angeles. He would talk to her right before he went to bed and after Dani had dinner. In the meantime, she would try to control her excitement at Reggie's house.

Regina Crawford is Dani's best friend. She lives four houses down the block. From the first day they met their friendship began. Their personalities fit together like two jigsaw puzzle pieces. Reggie was the first person Dani met after moving there from Brooklyn. On that day she saw Dani sitting alone on a school bench and came up to her. She asked, "What's your name?"

"Danielle," she replied.

"My name is Regina, but my friends call me Reggie."

"That's funny. My friends call me Dani." The girls giggled.

"I guess I won't be the only girl in school with a boy's nickname," said Reggie.

"Well, no one has called me Dani since I've been here," she confessed. "I don't have any friends yet." A little smile curled on Dani's lips.

"You do now," Reggie stated, and the girls laughed.

Dani walked passed her house and reached Reggie's. She took the three steps to the porch with one graceful leap. She started to knock on the door, but in between the first and second knocks came the voice of Reggie's mother. "Come on in, Dani." She stepped through the doorway. "Hi, Mrs. Crawford."

"Sweetheart, you know you don't have to knock. You're welcome here. You don't have to be so formal."

"I know. It's just that I'm used to always knocking before I enter somewhere. It's just a habit."

Mrs. Crawford turned around from the stove and faced Dani. "It's just your momma taught you proper manners. I wish more of Reggie's friends were as polite as you." Dani looked down at the floor, becoming embarrassed at the compliment. "I just want you to be comfortable in our house, Dani," expressed Mrs. Crawford.

"Oh, I am," said Dani.

"Good. Now why don't you go up and see Reggie. She's in her room."

Dani climbed the stairs and peered into Reggie's room. Reggie saw her head out of the corner of her eye. "Did my mom gush all over you again," asked Reggie in a teasing way. " I swear, if my mom could trade me for you she'd do it in a second. She's always asking me why I can't be more like you, Miss Perfect Princess Dani." Reggie said this with her hands forming a circle around her head, simulating a halo.

"Aw, cut it out," responded Dani, trying not to smile.

"Say, where were you after school?" Reggie asked. "I waited for you."

"Oh, I stopped at the library. I was looking for a book to use for my report in Mrs. Shaw's class. It's due next Monday, you know."

"Girl, don't even remind me," sighed Reggie. "I don't even want to think about it."

Dani turned to Reggie with eyebrows raised. "You're going to do it, aren't you?"

"Yeah, once I get started."

"Reg! You haven't even started?"

"Naw, I figured I'd talk you into writing it for me."

"You wish," Dani chuckled.

The girls talked for another half hour about school and boys, TV and boys, clothes and boys. Then, Dani rose and said she had to go. "I've got to get some homework done before tonight," Dani said.

"What's happening tonight?"

"Well, today is opening day, and..."

"Wait, wait, don't tell me. I've heard this one. It's opening day and your grandfather is going to call to talk about baseball and all the games you used to go to and who his favorite dead player was and..."

"Oh, come on, Reggie, it's not that bad. You know how close my grandfather and I are. We just like sharing the good times we've had. Baseball is something we both have in common."

"I know," Reggie confessed. "I was just teasing. To be honest, I'm a little jealous."

"Jealous, why?"

"Because you to have something to share. Even after you moved away from him, you're still close. I think that's pretty cool. My grandfather and I aren't that close. Really, I hardly know him. He's just some older relative I call my grandfather. He's just my mom's father. And I never knew my other grandfather. He died before I was born." Reggie paused, thinking about what she had just revealed to her friend. Both girls were staring at the floor. The silence was growing long and uncomfortable, so Reggie broke it.

"But, I still don't understand how you can get into baseball so much."

Dani smiled meekly, now looking at her shoes.

"Look, Reg. You're the only one outside my family who knows about my relationship with my grandfather and that I know so much about baseball. Can we kinda keep it that way?"

"You mean you don't want all the boys at school knowing you're a walking baseball encyclopedia?" Reggie asked, nudging her.

"No, it's not that. It's just personal, ya know? Baseball and my grandfather sort of go together. The less people who know about it, the more private it feels. Does that make any sense?"

"Yeah, it does. I guess I'm just stuck with this great secret for the rest of my life, huh?"

"Guess so," giggled Dani.

Chapter 3

Harold Rogers shuffled from the refrigerator carrying handfuls of supplies needed to complete his masterpiece. With Mrs. Rogers out shopping, he felt this the perfect time to sneak a between-meal snack. She wasn't there to warn him of spoiling his dinner, so he was going to take full advantage of the situation.

This masterpiece was a triple-decker sandwich, loaded with ham, turkey, tomatoes, and two kinds of cheese, piled two inches high on rye bread. He pressed down firmly on the super snack so he could slice it in half. Mayonnaise and mustard began to ooze down the sides of the bread. He loved when that happened.

He put the sandwich on the plate and carried it to the living room. Switching on the television, he settled into his recliner, ready to attack his creation. He rubbed his hands together excitedly and lifted half the sandwich to his mouth. Through the television speakers crackled the voice of Judge Judy, covering up the sounds of keys unlocking the back door. Mr. Rogers stared intently at the screen, smiling at the judge's sharp speech to the defendant, unaware of stirring in his own kitchen.

"Harold!" cried Mrs. Rogers.

"Wh...wh...what are you doing here?" asked Mr. Rogers, his mouth full of his masterpiece.

"I live here, remember?" She walked toward the recliner.

"What is that? she asked, pointing at the once-bitten sandwich.

"That? Well, it's, uh...well..."

"I can see it's a sandwich, silly old man." Edith Rogers shook her head, trying very hard not to let a smile sneak out. "I swear, I can't leave you alone for twenty minutes without you getting into trouble. Sometimes

I wonder if you're not a seven-year-old in a sixty-three-year-old's body."

"What trouble," Harold asked, grinning innocently. "I just wanted a snack."

"You know you waited for me to leave before you made that…that…thing, thinking you could sneak it past me. Besides, that's not a snack, it's a house," exclaimed Edith, now struggling to hold back a laugh.

"I thought it was a masterpiece," said Harold.

"You're only masterpiece is your wife," said Edith winking. Harold flashed that warm, disarming smile of his that made it hard for anyone to stay mad at him. Turning back toward the kitchen, Edith glanced at the sandwich again.

"My goodness," she screamed.

"What?" asked Harold.

"Look at all of that mayonnaise. Harold, you know the doctor said to ease up on eating stuff like that. You're heart can't keep taking what you keep giving it."

Harold had been to the doctor frequently the past four years. He had felt chest pains off and on. His right arm tingled for about five days. At the time the doctor said Harold had experienced a very mild heart attack. Hearing this scared Harold and Edith. He would have to take care of himself, getting more rest and watching what he ate. In the meantime, the two of them did not want to scare the family, so they didn't mention anything to anyone. They would bring it up at the right time to their son, Bobby. They did not, however, want to tell their granddaughter, Dani. Since her grandfather was doing well now, there seemed no reason to worry her.

"I know, honey, I'm sorry. You're right. I shouldn't be eating like this. I wasn't thinking. I guess I'm a little restless. I just can't wait to call Dani tonight."

"I know, dear, but she's still in school. You're going to have to wait."

"I know, but, well…what am I supposed to do in the meantime?"

"First of all, put that sandwich in the refrigerator. After that, why don't you go take a nap? You look tired. By the time you get up there will be a game on the radio and Dani will be home."

Harold picked up the sandwich and carried it to the kitchen. As he opened the refrigerator door he turned to Edith. "Do you think Dani looks forward to these phone calls on opening day as much as I do?"

"Oh, I'm sure she does, dear," Edith said. "I'm sure she does."

Chapter 4

D ani returned from Reggie's to begin her homework. Like Pop, she was restless also. She began her math homework for about fifteen minutes, got up to get something to drink, returned to her math homework for ten minutes, finished it, got up and changed her clothes, began reading a short story for English class, and put it down after two pages. Boy, was she restless.

She so looked forward to hearing from Pop. She thought about picking up the phone and calling him for a change, but she couldn't. Pop called her on opening day. That was the tradition. She wanted to keep this tradition, so she had to wait for him to call her. She wanted everything the same, every year. That's what she looked forward to, the security that it would happen the same way every year—forever.

Dani got up from the desk in her room and walked to the closet. She slowly opened the door and dropped to her knees. Reaching down, way in the back behind her shoes, Dani carefully pulled out a small, white rectangle box. She placed the box on the desk and untied the bright green yarn that held the lid on tight. Removing the lid, Dani stared down at the contents of her "treasure chest."

It wasn't a treasure chest like the ones in movies or television. Pirates with swords didn't try to steal it; no diamonds, jewels or gold lay inside. However, there were valuables in it just the same. They were things valuable to her, important things in her life she kept safe, secure, and sometimes secret.

Dani poked her fingers inside the box. She shuffled and flicked things around, looking for the one item she treasured most. She moved aside her baby ring her mother gave her when she was six months old. She took out the Valentine card from Tommy Morris, her boyfriend for two weeks in second grade. She lifted up a small picture of her parents' wedding day. Ah, there it was, at the bottom, her most prized possession. In its protective plastic cover was a card, *the* card. Jackie Robinson's rookie baseball card. Jackie Robinson, second baseman for the Brooklyn Dodgers. Jackie Robinson, the first African-American to play in the major leagues. All these things together made his card very valuable. Dani had heard it was worth quite a bit of money, but that was not why she kept it in her treasure chest as her most prized possession. It was valuable to Dani because Pop gave it to her.

It used to be Pop's most prized possession, too. He gave it to her after he started taking her to baseball games. Pop felt Dani would appreciate and respect the gift, and she did. As she grew older and more mature, Dani began to understand how important the card was to Pop and how much it meant to him. Not only was Jackie Robinson Pop's favorite player, he was also a hero and role model to him.

When Pop was a boy, African-Americans were not allowed to play in the major leagues. Discrimination was still powerful enough to keep them from playing in the "white" major leagues. They had to play in the Negro Leagues. When Jackie entered the major leagues in 1947, he became a symbol of change, of hope, and of pride to many. He was all of these things to Pop, being an African-American boy himself. The fact that he played for Pop's favorite team, the Brooklyn Dodgers, made him extra special.

Pop wanted to pass on this special part of baseball to Dani, to keep it alive through her. Early on, when Pop and Dani's baseball relationship began to grow, Pop saw the enjoyment and respect Dani had for baseball and their baseball relationship. He knew she would keep alive and value what the two of them shared. This is why Pop gave his most prized possession to Dani.

Dani stared at the card, turning it over in her fingers. In its plastic cover the card was in almost perfect condition. Pop must've really taken good care of this, she thought. In her heart, she swore to do the same.

She stared at the card for a moment longer, then carefully placed it back in her treasure chest, sliding it beneath all the other items so it safely rested at the bottom. After closing the lid, Dani tied the green yarn into a neat bow. She returned the box to the same place in the back of her closet. She wondered what Pop was doing right now. Probably, he was finishing dinner and helping grandma with the dishes. He would be settling into his favorite chair very soon, getting ready to make his traditional call. She knew it. There was no reason for her to be restless. He would be calling soon, probably any minute now. She had nothing to worry about.

Chapter 5

Edith Rogers was standing at the sink in the kitchen. She was peeling carrots for dinner. Carrots were Harold's favorite vegetable, so she thought she would make them for him after she scolded him about the sandwich. She wasn't mad at him, just concerned about his health. He knew better than that.

The pile of carrot shavings grew quickly in the sink. The steady *chick, chick, chick* of the carrot peeler was the only sound in the kitchen. Edith began to daydream about Dani while she worked. She could peel carrots and think about other things at the same time. She was a carrot-peeling pro, doing it for almost forty years for Harold. She knew she would get to talk to Dani tonight. Of course, she would have to wait for Dani to talk to her grandfather, the biggest conversation of the year, but she didn't mind. It was important to them, and she was glad. She knew Dani loved her, and she also knew Dani and her grandfather had a special relationship. She was thankful the two of them had each other, even though they were three thousand miles apart. My goodness, I miss Dani, she thought. Like Dani, Edith wished her son and Dani's mom, Patricia, could've worked things out. Even though she knew their divorce was probably for the best, she still wished things were different.

The carrots were all peeled. Still daydreaming about Dani, Edith gathered the pile of carrot peelings in both hands and began pushing them down the drain into the garbage disposal. She scraped up the last few pieces and guided them down the drain. As she reached for the switch to turn on the disposal, Edith heard a loud BANG!, snapping her out of the daydream. The noise startled her. She turned around, but no one was there. She slowly walked through the kitchen toward the hallway.

"Harold." No answer. She reached the hallway and stopped. "Harold." No answer again. She saw the light on in the bathroom. She started walking faster down the hall. "Harold." Still no answer. She reached the bathroom and stopped dead in the doorway, frozen by what she saw.

Harold lay on the floor on his back, knees curled up. His eyes were closed tight and his teeth clenched through his lips. Both hands were pressed on the left side of his chest, above his heart. A bottle of aspirin lay open on the floor by his shoulder, its contents spilled around his head like a broken strand of white pearls. Through his clenched teeth Harold forced out, "Edith," barely above a whisper.

"Harold!"

Chapter 6

The shrill of the telephone ringing jolted Bobby Rogers from a sound sleep. He laid down on the couch for a quick nap. That was two hours ago.

He rubbed his face to try and clear his grogginess. The ringing pierced his brain again, irritating him. He jumped off the couch to answer the phone before another ring came. In his haste he slammed his shin into the coffee table, sending shocks of pain up his leg. When he finally reached the phone, Bobby was not a happy man.

"Hello!" he barked into the receiver.

"Bobby, honey, is that you?"

"Yeah, ma, it's me. I'm sorry."

"Oh, Bobby! It's…it's…your father." Sobs and tears were choking off Edith's words, making it hard for her to speak.

"Dad? What's wrong?" Bobby asked, still trying to clear the sleepiness from his head and the pain in his leg.

"He's…he's…he's in the…hospital."

"Hospital!" Bobby snapped, his head quickly clearing. "What happened?"

"He's had a heart attack," sighed Edith. She now began telling Bobby for the first time about his father's health problem. It was almost a relief to finally reveal the secret to him.

"A heart attack! Oh, geez. Is he O.K.? When did this happen? Where is he?" Bobby rattled off questions to his mother, no longer groggy and sleepy, the pain in his leg forgotten, shock of the news jolting him to attention. Edith, although upset and scared, tried to answer all the questions.

"It's too early to tell about his condition, Bobby. He's in intensive care at King's County Hospital. I found him on the bathroom floor this evening. He was just...just.... She couldn't finish her sentence as fear and sadness rose through her and out her throat, cutting off her words. Tears flowed freely down her cheeks.

"It's O.K., ma. Dad's going to be all right." Bobby tried to sound strong for his mother, even though he didn't really feel that way inside. "Where are you?"

"I'm at the hospital," she sniffed.

"I'll be right there, mom. Don't worry." Bobby hung up the phone and stared at the receiver, frozen for a moment by the shock and disbelief. Dad had a heart attack, he thought. It still wasn't sinking in. He rubbed his face with both hands, dragging them up through his hair. He walked back to the couch and put on his shoes, tying them carelessly and in a hurry. He picked up his keys off the coffee table and hustled to the closet by the front door. He yanked out a jacket, making the hanger clank and rattle by the force of his pull. He reached for the doorknob when suddenly, his quick, hasty movements stopped. Dani, he thought. I've got to call Dani.

Chapter 7

Patricia Rogers was seated at the kitchen table sorting bills when the phone rang. She glanced at her watch when she rose from the chair. Wow. 7:45. This was much later than Pop usually called on opening day.

Patricia was well aware of his and Dani's opening day tradition. Thank goodness he finally called. Dani was going out of her mind, restlessly wandering around the house. She tried to keep Dani busy, giving her things to do to distract her from the waiting. Long ago, Dani cleared the table, washed, dried and put away the dinner dishes. She was now in the back of the house putting laundry in the dryer. As Patricia moved to the phone, she could hear Dani bounding and running toward the kitchen, her feet pounding noisily down the hall. Patricia placed her hand on the receiver and turned to the hallway, just in time to see Dani jump in to view, eyes wide, a big smile beaming across her face.

"Ha, ha. Got here first," Patricia said laughing, teasing Dani just a little. Dani didn't care, though. The phone *finally* rang.

"Hi, Harold," Patricia answered into the receiver, expecting to hear Pop's warm smooth voice.

"Trish, it's me."

"Bobby?" Patricia asked surprised.

"Yeah. Uh…how are you? How's Dani?"

"We're both fine." Patricia turned to Dani, whose expression changed from glee to disappointment. She realized it was dad and not Pop on the phone. "What's up? We haven't heard from you in a while."

Bobby paused. "Well…um…I…I have some bad news, real bad news."

Now Patricia paused, tensing up at what she was going to hear. "What is it?" she asked. Dani turned and went down the hall dejected, her shoulders slumped and her head down.

"It's dad," Bobby sighed. "He had a heart attack tonight."

"Oh my God," gasped Patricia, her free hand covering her mouth. "Is he all right?"

"We don't know yet. It's too early to tell. I...I just thought of Dani. I thought she should know."

"Yes, you're right. Oh, dear. This will crush her." Patricia took a long deep breath and rubbed her forehead, knowing what this news would do to Dani. "Let me get her on the line."

"No, no!" cried Bobby. "I can't tell her. Not in my condition. I can't deal with that right now. I called wanting to tell her, but I just can't. You tell her."

"Oh, great!" Patricia snapped. "Once again, Bobby, you can't take responsibility, leaving me to do all the dirty work. Some things never change."

"Trish, please. Let's not argue now. I'm a wreck. I know what this will do to Dani. There's no way I can deal with that right now. I can barely deal with it myself. Please?"

Patricia knew this was hard for Bobby. "O.K., O.K. I'll tell her," she said giving in, not knowing how she would do it.

"Thanks. I'll keep in touch with you, let you know when I have some news."

"Yes, please. Oh, and Bobby...I'm so sorry."

Bobby closed his eyes. "Yeah, me too."

Chapter 8

Patricia slowly hung up the phone, rocked by what she just heard. Poor Harold, I hope he'll be O.K., she thought. Just because she wasn't married to their son anymore didn't mean she no longer cared about them. She did care about them, very much. They were always good to her, and they adored Dani. She missed them too. She said a silent prayer for Harold.

When Patricia opened her eyes, the dread of what she had to do next soaked deep inside her, making a knot in her stomach the size of a grapefruit. She had to tell Dani. She walked down the hall wondering what she would say, how she would say it. Dani was in her room, the laundry already in the dryer. Patricia peeked her head in the doorway, finding Dani lying on her bed, a magazine in front of her face.

"Dani," she said softly.

"Does dad want to talk to me?" Dani asked, sitting up on the bed.

"No, dear. Well…yes, he did, but he couldn't."

"Why?" Dani and her mom had always been honest and open with each other. The only other time she had this much trouble talking to Dani was when she had to explain the marriage separation.

"Sweetheart, I have something to tell you, but I don't know how to say it. So, I'm just going to spit it out." She took a deep breath through her nose and blew it out loudly through her mouth. Hearing this told Dani something really must be wrong.

"Baby, Pop had a heart attack tonight."

Dani heard the words her mother said, but she didn't really understand at first. The words seemed to rattle and jumble around in her brain, not making sense. In her mind, Dani began to repeat the words she heard: Pop had a heart attack. Pop had a heart attack. Pop had a heart attack...POP HAD A HEART ATTACK!

What her mother said finally came into focus. Dani's breathing stopped, her eyes grew wide, her mouth froze, half-open, like she was about to say something but couldn't. She just stared back at her mother, silent.

"Dani, honey, did you hear me?" Patricia asked her daughter gently. Dani still couldn't speak. She just stared back at her mother. Tears puddled up in her eyes until they became too full, and the tears rolled down her cheeks. She slowly closed her mouth and whispered..."No." Patricia sat next to her on the bed.

"No," Dani said again, a little more loudly. Patricia moved closer to her daughter and put her arms around her.

"Noooo!" Dani screamed and buried her head between her mother's neck and shoulder, tears flowing freely from her eyes into her mother's blouse.

Dani sobbed on her mother for several minutes. Patricia said nothing, slowing rocking Dani back and forth. Finally, Dani spoke, pulling her head away from her mother. "Is he going to be all right?" she asked through sniffs and sobs.

"We don't know yet," her mother replied, looking deeply and honestly into Dani's eyes. "It's too early to know anything. He's at the hospital now." Dani looked down, now knowing why Pop didn't call. He couldn't. "I know this is very hard for you right now. I'll leave so you can be alone, if you want."

"O.K., mom," Dani said, her mind locked on Pop.

Patricia rose from the bed and walked to the doorway. She stopped and turned toward her daughter, seeing her angel staring at the floor, shattered, afraid, and alone. Patricia's heart was breaking too, seeing Dani like this, wanting to take all her pain away if she could.

"I'll be in the other room if you need me, baby," she said weakly, not knowing what else to say. Dani said nothing. Her thoughts were not in her bedroom. They were three thousand miles away.

Chapter 9

Dani hardly slept that night, maybe a couple of hours. She went back and forth between thinking and crying, staring at the ceiling and wiping her eyes. Would Pop be O.K.? He had to be O.K., she kept rolling in her mind.

She also felt foolish and guilty for her thoughts last night. She was so restless and worried that Pop was late in calling her. She was disappointed that his call hadn't come and that she had to wait. Now she had to worry about something far bigger and more serious—Pop's health. Would he be all right? Would he ever call again? She stopped her thoughts right there.

Yes, he would be O.K. Everything was going to be fine, she told herself, trying to hide the negative thoughts so she couldn't hear them.

Dani dragged herself out of bed after her alarm clock woke her. She was so tired. She rubbed her face as she walked into the kitchen. Her mom was already there, laying slices of bread on the counter.

"I'm making a tuna sandwich for lunch. Want one too?"

"Yeah, I guess so.

"Aren't you going to have breakfast?" her mother asked.

"I'm not hungry," Dani sighed.

"Sweetie, I know you're not happy right now. I know you're tired. I can tell by looking at you that you probably didn't sleep much last night. But, you still should have something for breakfast. At least have some juice."

Dani opened the refrigerator door without saying a word. She pulled out a carton of orange juice and carried it to the cupboard where the glasses were.

After pouring herself half a glass, she replaced the carton and sat at the table, staring at the glass of juice in front of her. She was looking at it but not really seeing it. Her mind was a million miles away.

"Dani, honey, I put your sandwich in a bag. Don't forget it."

"O.K., mom," she said, barely hearing her mother. Patricia turned and saw the sad, blank look on her daughter's face. She walked over to the table and bent down next to Dani. "Dad's going to call when he has some news. Everything's going to be all right." She brushed some hair away from Dani's eyes and kissed her on the forehead. "You'll see. Everything will work out." Dani managed a half-smile but said nothing.

Patricia rose up and walked to the door, picking up her keys on the way. "I'll see you when I get home," she said before closing the door on her way to work. Dani sat at the table, juice still in front of her, untouched. She hoped her mother was right, that everything would be all right.

The hot shower helped Dani wake up, the fuzziness in her head began to clear. As she stood under the spray she tried to focus on the telephone, listening for the ring, just in case her father called with some news on Pop. It's strange, she thought. Just yesterday she was waiting all day for Pop to call. Now, she's waiting for her dad to call. It seemed to her that for the past sixteen hours her life had been tied to that phone. She felt helpless, powerless, not in control. She wasn't used to these feelings, and she didn't like it. If only she could *do* something so she didn't feel this way. But what...what?

The shower cleared Dani's head, but the empty feeling remained. She dressed and sat at the edge of her bed, almost frozen. Tired. She couldn't remember when she had felt so tired. The combination of getting almost no sleep and the stress of thinking about Pop was weighing down on her like snow on the branches of trees, ready to break. She was drained and exhausted.

Five minutes. I'll just lay down for five minutes, she thought. Then I'll leave for school.

Just as her head hit the pillow, Dani was fast asleep.

Chapter 10

Edith and Bobby sat in chairs pulled up to Harold's bed. He was still unconscious and had been since the ambulance ride from home to the hospital. The doctor said his vital signs were O.K. for now, but they had to be watched closely. Harold was hooked up to a heart monitor that kept track of his heartbeats and how strong they were. The beats were steady, but they were weaker than normal. Because Harold was unconscious, the doctors could not tell at this time about any damage the heart attack may have caused. They were still running tests.

Edith's hand rested on Bobby's knee. His hand was on hers for comfort. "Mom, why don't you go home and get some rest? I'll stay with him for a while. You've been here since last night. You must be tired."

"No, I can't go," she said, staring at Harold. I'll be even more restless sitting at home waiting. I'd rather stay here. This waiting and wondering what's going to happen is so hard, but if I have to do it, I want to do it near your father."

A long silence fell between the two of them, their hands still connecting them. Bobby finally broke the quiet with a question. "Ma, why didn't you tell me before about dad's heart problem? Why keep it a secret?"

"I didn't want to worry you. Since the other heart attack was a minor one, and he came out of it all right, we didn't want to upset anyone. We didn't even tell Dani and Patricia. You were going through the separation at the time, and that was hard on all of you. We felt it best to keep it quiet. I probably should have said something to you, well, sometime. It just seemed like the right thing to do at the time. We were just trying to protect you."

"I know, ma, I know. This was just such a shock. It, it…scared me."

"I'm scared too, honey," Edith confessed as she buried her face in her free hand; the other still on Bobby's leg.

Dani's sleep was heavy and deep. Vivid dreams danced through her mind. Pop's face jumped into view many times, usually smiling. She was remembering how he looked when she used to see him often. An image of her and Pop playing cards at the kitchen table appeared. She pictured the two of them watching TV together and sitting on the front steps at night, looking at the moon and watching cars go by. Visions came from the baseball park, where they sat in the sun and watched the game, and talked, and giggled, and ate, and giggled some more. All these pleasant dreams ran together, one right after the other, a collage of happy times shared between her and Pop.

Image after image looped together, until…a vision appeared that broke the loop. In Dani's dream she saw Pop lying on a bed, his eyes closed. "Pop," she calls out, trying to wake him. She moves closer to the bed and calls out a little louder. No response. Dani moves right next to him and gently shakes his shoulder. "Pop, wake up," she calls again. Nothing. She shakes him even harder, repeating his name over and over. He doesn't move. "Pop!" she yells. "Please open your eyes! Pop!"

Dani jolted awake from her dream, her body coated in a thin film of perspiration. Her eyes stared straight up at the ceiling in fear, panic and desperation. "Oh, God," she whispered. "This can't happen. Pop can't go." Dani was still shaking from the effects of the dream as tears welled up in her eyes and rolled down each side of her face. Her breath came in short gasps as the possibility of Pop dying hit her like a slap in the face. Her fear, panic and desperation now racing through her.

No, it can't be like this, she thought. I can't lose Pop. I haven't even seen him in so long. But, what if it's true? What if he does die.? I have to see him, at least one more time. I just *have* to.

Dani lay on the bed a while longer, still staring at the ceiling. Her mind focused on her new goal—to see Pop. After that dream she knew that's what she had to do. She would wait until mom came home from work and ask if she could take her to New York. Mom cared for Pop, she thought to herself. She would probably want to see him too.

Chapter 11

Honestly, Dani, there's just no way we can go."

"But mom," Dani pleaded, "what if something happens to Pop? I'd never see him again." Dani was not one who whined, even as a small child. She had always been mature for her age. But now, she sounded like a little girl. Her words came out in a higher pitched tone with little whimpers and gasps, as if there were tears in her voice. Her mother heard and saw this. She felt terrible seeing her daughter like this.

"I know this is hard on you. It's hard on me too. But, there's no way we can go right now. I can't take the time off of work, and even if I could, I can't afford two round-trip tickets to New York. I'm sorry, sweetheart, but I just can't do it."

Everything her mother said Dani heard and understood, but it still wasn't good enough. It still didn't get her to Pop. It still left her feeling empty and helpless.

"Please, mom," Dani begged. "I have to see him."

"I'm sorry, honey," Patricia confessed, almost in tears herself, "but we just can't." Dani turned and ran to her bedroom, tears of frustration blurring her vision as she closed the door and leaped on her bed, burying her face in the pillows. Dani now cried freely. Sobs, gasps, and tears gushed out from deep inside her like water through a broken dam. The emotions from the last two days mixed together in one big rush and release. She felt defeated, wanting so desperately to see Pop but having no way to do so.

Patricia heard Dani's crying through the door. It was tearing at her heart to tell Dani no. She knew how important Pop was to her, how close they were even though they lived so far apart. She wanted to go in and comfort her but didn't know what to say. She moved toward the door then stopped. No, she thought. Not now. I'll leave Dani alone for a while. I'll go in later and talk to her. Patricia turned and went back to the kitchen, leaving the sounds of Dani's crying hanging in the air behind her.

Three thousand miles away in King's County Hospital, Brooklyn, Harold Rogers lay motionless on the bed, alone. Visiting hours were over. Edith and Bobby had recently left. Bobby finally talked his mother into going home and getting some rest. To keep her from being alone, he would stay at her house.

Harold had still not regained consciousness.

Two hours later, Dani was still in her room on the bed. The loud, strenuous crying had stopped, but Dani was feeling no better. She was tired and miserable. She was on her back, staring at the ceiling, her mother's words still ringing in her head: "I can't get off work…I can't afford two round-trip tickets…I can't get off work…I can't afford two round-trip tickets…." Again and again her mother's voice repeated this in her mind, each time making Dani feel worse and more helpless. Work; can't afford two; work; can't afford two; can't afford—*two.*

Dani's mind stopped racing and repeating. The only word that registered now was *two.* Two tickets. Hey, Dani thought, if mom can't afford two tickets, what about one? Yeah, that's it! If I can get mom to let me go alone, maybe there is a chance I can see Pop!

Dani's feelings of gloom and depression began to clear. She finally had some hope. She took in a deep breath and blew it out in a sigh of relief, feeling better now than she had over the last couple of days. Now all she had to do was convince her mom to let her go alone. That would be no easy task. She would have to do some fancy talking and persuading, maybe even some tears, to get mom to see things her way. This could be tough.

Dani turned on her side, pulling her knees up to her chest, hugging them. How would she do it? How could she get her mom to let her go alone? She was absorbed, deep in thought, when a soft knock on her door broke her concentration.

"Dani, honey, can we talk?" came her mother's voice from the other side of the door.

"Uh, yeah, sure mom. Come in." Oh, oh, Dani thought. I don't know what to say yet. I'm not ready. I don't have it figured out.

Patricia's face peeked through the doorway, a soft smile on her face. "Hi. How are you feeling?"

"I left your note for school on the counter in the kitchen." Dani told her mom how she fell asleep and missed school. Mom was supportive. She knew how upset and tired Dani was. She wasn't mad at all.

"Thanks, mom." Dani sat there for a moment wondering what to do. She noticed that mom seemed to be in a good mood (considering all that happened), a smile on her face, checking on her to see how she was.

Patricia broke the silence. "Dani, I know you were upset earlier. Do you want to talk about anything?"

"Uh, well, mom," Dani stammered. Oh boy. I guess this is it, she thought. I might as well get it over with now. Dani got up from her bed and walked down the hall to the kitchen. She was going to retrieve the note for school her mom wrote, but she was also stalling. She was trying to collect her thoughts, to organize in her mind what she was going to say. Her mom followed behind.

"Dani, what is it?" she asked calmly. They were both in the kitchen now. Dani took a deep breath.

"You said that we couldn't go because you couldn't get off work and you couldn't afford two tickets. Well, what if…um, what if?" Dani stuttered, fumbled her words. She was nervous about asking. She was afraid to ask, afraid of what mom might say. This was her last hope, and she knew it.

"What is it, sweetheart," her mom asked. Dani took a deep breath, closing her eyes to try to relax. She concentrated on just getting the question out.

"Mom, what if, instead of buying two plane tickets, you get just one— for me?" Dani held her breath, waiting for the answer. Patricia's eyes softened, her eyebrows arched up as a sad expression began to creep across her face.

"Oh, Dani, I can't send you across the country by yourself. I know this is important to you, but I just don't think that's a good idea. Besides, even one ticket is still quite a bit of money."

Dani stood frozen, a lump in her throat that felt like a golf ball. Her mouth was open, but no sound came out—yet. A dark, whirlpool feeling began churning deep in her stomach, rising slowly inside her. It crawled up her chest and to her throat. All at once, a burst of emotion mixed with words of desperation flew out of her mouth, almost beyond her control: "Mom, please let me go! It's my only chance, I can handle it, I can go by myself, I can do it, I'll do everything, I'll take homework with me, I'll call dad to meet me, I'il arrange everything, I'll even pay for it myself. Please, mom!"

Patricia stood there for a long time as Dani's rapid-fire words hung in the air like smoke. She stared at her daughter, almost looking inside her, seeing an exhausted little girl. Her baby. She knew, though, that Dani wasn't that little anymore. She was thirteen and quite mature for her age. She had always felt lucky for and proud of her responsible daughter. Still, she felt uneasy about letting her travel alone.

Dani said something about paying for it herself, Patricia thought. It was quite a bit of money for a thirteen-year-old to come up with. Deep down, she didn't think Dani could do it. However, coming up with the money would show more maturity and responsibility. This gave Patricia an idea. She looked at her daughter a long time before responding.

"Tell you what, Dani. I'm not really comfortable with you going alone. But, I'm going to make you a deal." Dani's eyes grew bigger, her breath stopped in anticipation. "If you arrange everything *and* you come up with the money yourself, that will show me you're responsible enough to go."

Dani heard her mother's words, but it took a moment for them to sink in. She couldn't believe it. Dd her mother just say she could go? Yes! Yes, she did! Dani's eyes grew even bigger as a smile streaked across her face. "Oh, thank you, mom! Thank you!" Dani squealed, leaping toward her mother, wrapping her arms around her neck. Dani was close to tears, again, but this time they were tears of joy.

Dani raced across the hall to her room. She felt so light and relieved it seemed her feet barely touched the ground, like she was walking on air.

Patricia watched her scamper away with mixed feelings. She was glad to see Dani so happy, but did she do the right thing? Would Dani be disappointed even more if she could not go after all? She would have to just wait and see.

Chapter 12

Bursting through the doorway of her room, Dani lunged on her bed faced-down, arms stuck straight out from her body as if she were flying. What a relief she felt, a heavy weight lifted from her body. She did it! Mom's going to let her go! She almost couldn't believe it.

Dani didn't move for a while. It felt good to spread out, letting the tension and stress that had been inside her melt out of her body. She had felt so bad and low about Pop that she wondered if she would ever feel good again. Now she knew she could.

After a few more minutes of enjoying her peace, a thought came to Dani that made the smile on her face fade away. Thinking about seeing Pop made her happy. However, the fact was he was still sick, real sick. Her thoughts changed from seeing him to what he would be like when she did see him. Would he be able to talk to her? Would she be frightened when she saw him? Would she cry? All these questions rushed through her mind at once. The joy of being able to see him was quickly changing to serious concern. How *is* he? she asked herself.

Harold turned his head slightly in his dark hospital room. Today, his conditioned had not worsened, but it had not improved either. His fingertips curled into his palm a few times, making soft, gentle fists, his fingers lightly scratching across the blanket.

For the first time in hours, Harold's lips moved. A sound so soft, maybe not even enough to be called a whisper, floated from his throat and disappeared just past his lips, lost in the silent room. *"Daaanii."*

His fingers curled into his palm just a little tighter.

Still lying on her bed, Dani's thoughts focused on Pop. His face, his illness, their good times together, missing him, all these images flashed before her eyes, smothering the joyous feelings she had only minutes before when her mother said she could go. She needed to feel better. She needed to direct her thoughts on something else, put her mind to work on something useful.

Dani's brain clicked on something that caught her attention. This new thought was big enough to distract her from thinking about Pop. In fact, this new idea—this problem—could keep her from seeing Pop at all. How was she going to afford to fly to New York to see him? This would certainly distract her. This was big.

The gears in Dani's brain began to turn, thinking hard about how she would solve this problem. She had a little bit of money saved up from birthdays and babysitting, but she was sure it wasn't nearly enough. If mom said she could not afford it right now, it must be expensive.

Come on, Dani, think, she told herself. She couldn't borrow the money from anyone. She wouldn't do anything illegal or wrong to get the money, no matter how badly she wanted to see Pop. She just couldn't. That left just one thing. She would have to sell something, or some *things*.

Dani sat up on her bed cross-legged, elbows on knees, hands made into fists under her chin. She did her best thinking this way. She stared at the floor, but she wasn't really seeing it. Her mind was elsewhere, racing, trying to imagine everything she had that she could possibly sell. She began a mental list of her belongings. Her clothes? Maybe she could sell a few, but that wouldn't raise much money. Some books and cassette tapes, maybe some CD's? No, same thing, just a few bucks. Some toys and games? Well, a few dollars there, but still way short.

Hey, she thought, what if I combined all those things together? No, that wouldn't work either. It was a good idea, and the combined total of all the items would help, but how would she organize it? She may not have time to put together a kind of garage sale. She would probably have to wait until the weekend to do it, and Pop might not be…no. She would not think like that. No.

Still, she wanted the money as quickly as possible. She would leave right now if she could. Even though it may be a possibility, waiting that long to see him was not what she wanted. She needed a plan to get the money now.

Restlessly, Dani walked to her closet and flung open the doors. Her eyes searched and her mind raced frantically. What did she have? What could she use? Her eyes scanned across all the items in her closet, but her brain would not lock on to anything particular.

Dani walked to her bed and plopped down in frustration. She sat and stared at the open closet. It looked full, but right now it seemed empty. A sigh escaped from her chest. How could she see Pop if she couldn't figure out how to get there? "Oh, Pop," she said aloud, "what am I going to do?"

His face glided across her mind, over and over Dani sank into a deep daydream. She saw Pop laughing; she saw him walking with her hand-in-hand; she saw him with her in the stands at a baseball game; she saw…wait a minute. Images of Pop and baseball began to fill her thoughts. Pop and baseball were inseparable, united as always in her mind. She could not think about baseball without thinking about Pop. All her wonderful memories of both flashed before her. They seemed so real. Dani felt she could almost reach out and touch Pop. The images were pulling at her, tugging at her brain, at her emotions. She just floated, drifted, daydreaming, just….

The images stopped just as quickly as they began. Dani sat on the edge of her bed, straight and rigid, like a soldier snapping to attention. She arose from the bed and walked to the closet. Once again, Dani flung the doors open, but this time she had a purpose, a direction, a goal. Reaching behind her shoes she pulled out the white box with the bright green ribbon—her treasure chest.

As if they had a mind of their own, Dani's fingers connected with the object at the bottom of the box. Two fingers carefully grasped the thin, smooth rectangle. Dani pulled it out and stared at it. There it was…the card.

Chapter 13

It was perfect. The clear, glossy, plastic case surrounded the perfect, like new Jackie Robinson rookie card; perfect because the case protected it for so many years; perfect because Dani took such good care of it; perfect because he was Pop's favorite player; perfect because Pop gave it to her.

The was also the perfect, well, only solution she could think of to see Pop. Dani knew it was valuable, several hundred dollars as she remembered. Selling this card could give her enough money to buy the airline ticket.

Dani stared at the card. She lightly brushed her fingers across the case's shiny surface. There is was, the possible solution to her problem. However, Dani was not as excited as one might think. There was no jumping for joy, no tears of happiness of relief, not even a smile. Dani gazed down at the card in serious thought. Could she sell it? Could she give up the thing that represented the wonderful relationship she had with Pop? Could she part with her most prized possession? Dani had to think clearly. She could not remember a more important decision she had to make.

Dani sat at her desk finishing up some homework. Being absent from school today left her with a few things to finish.

Dinner had been quiet. She did not reveal to mom her possible plan of selling the card. She still was not sure. What else could she do? It seemed like the only way to be able to see him. However, it was such a big piece of her, of Pop, of them. She had never dreamed of giving up the card before. It was the symbol of their relationship.

Dani struggled to complete the last few algebra problems on the page. She was struggling to stay focused. Pop's face kept creeping into her mind, making it hard to concentrate. Algebra was supposed to help you think clearly and logically. Right now, though, Dani's thoughts were jumbled, bouncing from Pop to the card to her homework.

Finally, Dani finished her algebra ten minutes later. She was now free to sort out her much tougher problem. She decided to take a lesson from her homework, to solve her problem by thinking clearly and logically. Instead of joining Pop and the card together, Dani decided to separate them, put them on opposite sides, like isolating the variable in algebra. That way, she could think of each individually.

Dani moved to her bed. She laid on her back, hands clasped behind her head, staring at the ceiling. She let her mind drift. Her thoughts swirled around the Jackie Robinson rookie card and what it meant to her.

The card was special—no doubt about that. Pop gave it to her. It was important to him, probably *his* most prized possession, Dani thought. The fact that he trusted her with it and gave her something so special and valuable to him made her appreciate the card even more. It was something physical that connected her to Pop, something she could touch, feel, and hold to remind her of him. She felt it was the most important thing she had.

Now Dani let her mind drift to Pop. This was easy and natural, because she thought of him a lot, especially over the last couple of days. Thinking of him made her smile, feel warm, feel happy. Next to mom, he was the most important person in her life. She was realizing again that he was even more important to her than her father. Oh, she loved dad, of course. She always would. She was just closer to Pop, connected more with him, shared more with him. He brought joy to her life, not just with baseball, but everything. Dani smiled as she thought about Pop, feeling the joy thinking about him gave her. He was so special, even more special than…than the card.

Dani's heart swelled and her mind opened up, like curtains being pulled open to let in the light. That's the answer, she thought to herself. True, the card was her most prized possession, but it was just a thing, an object. Pop was a person, a person she loved very much. She needed to see him. If something happened to Pop and she didn't take this opportunity to see him, she would never forgive herself. Never.

That was it. She would do it. Now she needed a plan to sell it, and quickly.

Chapter 14

Regina was reclining on her bed. She was leaning up against the headboard, her face buried in the latest copy of *Teen* magazine. She heard the phone ring downstairs but knew her mother would answer it. She continued flipping through the pages of the magazine until her mother's voice snapped her out of her peaceful relaxation.

"Reggie, telephone!"

She groaned aloud. "Uhh. Can't a girl get any time to herself?" Crawling off the bed she staggered down the hall to the stairs. "This better be good," she mumbled through a yawn. "It better be a boy." Reggie walked to the kitchen and picked up the receiver with a touch of curiosity. "Hello."

"Hi, Reg, it's me."

"Oh, hi Dani," Reggie sighed, a tone of disappointment in her voice.

"Gee, that's some greeting. What's wrong with you?" Dani asked.

"Oh, nothing. I was hoping you were a boy."

"Well, sorry to disappoint you," Dani kidded. "Look, Reg, I need to talk. Can you come over?"

"Sure. Is everything alright? You weren't at school."

"Well, I don't know," said Dani meekly. Reggie noticed the tone in Dani's voice and became concerned. It wasn't like Dani to sound meek and insecure. She was the most confident person Reggie knew.

"I'm on my way," she said, and was out the door.

Within two minutes the two girls were on Dani's bed, face-to-face. Reggie saw how tired Dani looked, so she started the conversation to break the ice.

"I hope this is important. I could be missing any number of calls from boys right now." Reggie said this in her usual teasing, kidding way, but all she received from Dani was a thin, weak grin, barely a curl of the lips.

"Whoa," Reggie uttered, "this seems serious. Talk to me, girl. You know you can tell me anything." Dani knew this too. The two girls confided in each other all the time. They shared secrets, dreams, feelings—personal things. They trusted each other. Reggie was the only friend Dani would share this with.

Dani sighed deeply. "Well, it's Pop."

"Oh, yeah," Reggie inserted. "How did that first day of baseball thing of yours go?"

"It didn't," Dani replied. She began to tell Reggie of the previous day's events, slowly at first, but with more ease the more she told. Reggie sat quietly, letting Dani release her emotions about her grandfather. After a long silence, Reggie reached over and hugged Dani for comfort.

"I'm so sorry, Dani. I know how close you two are. It's too bad he's so far away.

Dani pulled away from the embrace. "Well, I kind of have a plan, maybe."

Chapter 15

The bell rang announcing the end of school. Dani met Reggie in front of her class. Instead of walking home, the two girls were catching the city bus to the mall. Dani did indeed have a plan.

She came up with it after Reggie had left last night. She called several airlines to get round-trip ticket prices from Los Angeles to New York. All of them were several hundred dollars. The cheapest she found was $525. Wow! That was a lot of money to Dani. She had a little bit saved up from babysitting, but not nearly that much. She would have to see how much she could get for the card to cover the cost.

She and Reggie would go to the mall, making two stops. First, the bookstore, where they also sell magazines. The second stop would be the hobby shop. In there comic books and sports cards were bought and sold.

Once on the bus, Dani was quiet, deep in thought. Reggie, never one to stay quiet for long, had to break the silence.

"By the way, Dani, why are we going to the mall? Not that I'm complaining, of course. You know me, say the word "mall" and I'm the first one there. But, what's up? After what you told me last night I figured the last thing you'd want to do is shop."

"We're not shopping. This is part of my plan."

"Oh, the plan," remarked Reggie. "I still can't believe you're thinking of selling the card. I couldn't imagine having to make that decision."

"Yeah, tell me about it," Dani added. "I have a knot in my stomach just thinking about it."

The girls rode in silence a few minutes until their stop. As they stepped off the bus Reggie stated, "Last night you asked for my help. Well, how can I help?"

"You're helping me now."

Reggie looked confused. "What do you mean?"

"Selling this card to see my sick grandfather is the hardest thing I've had to do. I can't do it alone. I need my best friend with me."

Reggie smiled and wrapped her arm around Dani's neck. She pressed their heads together so their foreheads lightly touched. She locked on Dani's eyes. "I'm here for you, Dani," confided Reggie. "I'm here."

The bookstore was quiet except for the soft classical music floating down from the store's sound system. A few customers strolled among the aisles. Dani and Reggie were alone in front of the magazine rack at the front of the store.

"Are you sure you know what you're looking for?" Reggie asked.

"Yeah, the magazine is called *Beckett*. Help me look."

"What's in it?"

"It shows the value of sports trading cards based on their condition."

"Uh…O.K., but how do you know this? I swear you're the only girl in the city who knows this."

"My grandfather told me about it. I looked through one once before, and I've seen it on the shelf here in the past."

"How much do you think the card is worth?"

"I'm not sure exactly. I never looked it up." Dani sighed deeply. "I never thought I'd be selling it."

"Do you think it's worth enough to buy an airline ticket?"

"I hope so."

Dani found the magazine on the bottom shelf and picked it up. She flipped through the pages briskly while Reggie peered over her shoulder. Each page listed names of players and sets of cards. They were listed in groups by the brand of card and the year they were made. To the right of each name were two prices—the low and high values. Each card could be bought or sold for an amount somewhere between the low and high values, depending on the card's condition; the better condition a card is in, the more it is worth.

To Dani, this vast collection of names, numbers, and information made sense. To Reggie, it was an overwhelming mountain of gibberish, about as understandable as ancient Greek.

Dani continued to flip pages, quickly scanning each, looking for the brand and year of the card. Reggie watched in bewilderment, her eyes glazing over in amazement and confusion as pages loaded with data whizzed by, only to be followed by a new page just as amazing and confusing.

A moment later Dani's frenzied flipping halted abruptly. She had found the heading for the brand of card she had, 1949 Bowman. Dani's finger slid down the column of names. She found "Jackie Robinson RC", his rookie card. It was a fairly rare card, and definitely an old one. Dani's particular card was in near perfect condition. Pop had always kept it protected, and so did she.

Her finger stopped underneath "Jackie Robinson" then slid across the column to the card's value. Dani gasped, paused, blinked, and stared at it some more.

"What! What! What is it? How much?" Reggie wailed impatiently. "Don't just stand there with your mouth open like a fish. Tell me!"

"I…I…I can't believe it," squeaked Dani.

"Can't believe what?" Reggie asked. Not knowing what was going she looked at Dani's face for a clue. Dani's eyes were watering, her eyelashes barely able to hold in the tears.

"Oh no," sighed Reggie, seeing her face, "it's that bad?"

"No, Reg," Dani whispered breathlessly, "it's that good." The low value list next to Jackie Robinson's name was $700.

Chapter 16

Bobby sat alone in the busy hospital cafeteria. It was dinnertime, and many of the tables were occupied, mostly by hospital employees. He tried to convince his mother to get something to eat, but she refused, saying she wasn't hungry. He would bring her something anyway.

Actually, being alone is what Bobby needed right now. He was thinking about his father. The initial shock of the news was gone, but he still wondered if his father would be well. He had thought all along his father was in good health until his mother broke the news to him over the phone. He had no idea and was totally unprepared for this.

He also felt for Dani. He knew this must be killing her. Dani and his father were a team. Being so far away from him was probably making her pain ten times worse. His heart went out to her.

He also felt badly about not talking to Dani himself when he called. Making Patricia do it was cowardly. He seemed to be good at that—finding the easy way out of situations instead of doing the right thing. He needed to call Dani back, talk to her directly. When he had more information about Dad he would call. He thought briefly about what he might tell her. It would be hard for him, but he needed to start doing the right thing. He might as well start with his daughter.

Dani blinked furiously trying to pump the tears from her eyes. She wanted to make sure the blurred vision from her tears wasn't playing tricks on her eyes. There it was, staring right back at her: $700. That meant she could expect to get at least that much for the card. Dani blossomed a smile and released a sigh that seemed to start at her toes and shoot through her body and out her mouth. It was as if a stack of bricks had been taken off her shoulders. What a relief!

Her finger was still pointing at the price column as Reggie gazed over her shoulder in amazement.

"It's worth *that* much? Incredible! I would've never guessed."

"Yeah, it is pretty cool, isn't it," Dani confessed.

"So, what now?"

"We're going across the mall to the card shop. Let's see how much they'll give me for it."

The girls hustled across the mall. Normally, they would never travel so fast when in the mall; they might miss some of the sights, namely boys. Reggie was especially good at strolling through the mall at a leisurely pace. This was her territory.

Today, however, was different. Reggie knew this, knew the seriousness of their trek to the card store.

She was not at the mall to get attention for herself. She was there for Dani. Each step closer to the store must be torture for her, Reggie thought, like she's walking uphill. This is not about me. It's about my best friend having to do something she never dreamed she would have to do.

The girls walked in silence across the stretch of shiny hexagon tiles that made up the mall's floor. Reggie's head was down, watching the tiles whiz by under their rapid pace. Dani's gaze was straight ahead, her face serious, firm, determined. She took a deep breath as she saw the entrance to the card shop up ahead. Her pace slowed slightly as she reached into her purse dangling at her hip. She stopped at the store's entrance as she removed the plastic encased card.

"Well, here we are," said Dani, a weak, unsure smile on her face.

"Yep, here we are." Reggie, always free with her words, knew nothing else to say.

Dani took the first step forward. "Let's get this over with." The girls entered the card shop, Reggie trailing behind. Walking toward the back of the store they saw a man, maybe fifty years old, standing behind a glass display counter. On the way to the back of the store the girls passed several glass cases on either side, their shelves filled with sports cards on display; baseball, football, basketball, and hockey players staring toward the ceiling from their protective shelter, frozen in time. Posters, jerseys, pictures, some autographed, some not, cluttered the walls of the store, so much so that the color of the walls was hard to identify. The eyes were treated to so much it was hard to focus on any one thing. Dani barely noticed the visual show, her mind set on the task at hand. Reggie, however, gawked in wonder, mouth open wide and eyes even wider. She stood in the middle of the store turning slowly in a circle, trying to take everything in. This was all new to her, a different world.

When Dani reached the counter the man looked up from his papers. He smiled. "What can I do for you today?"

His smile helped, but Dani was still nervous.

"I…uh…have this card I…uh…want to sell." *Want* really wasn't the right word. She needed to sell it. But Dani didn't say "need" because whoever would buy the card may get the idea that she was desperate and not give her the best price. She had rehearsed this in her mind walking silently from the book store to the card shop.

"Do you have it with you?" the man asked pleasantly.

"Yes," Dani replied meekly. She held up the card one final time to take a last long look. This card, safely stored away in her treasure chest all this time, the symbol of the bond between her and Pop, was about to be handed over to a stranger. She felt tears wanting to rise up and overflow her eyes, but she held them in. She couldn't control the knot in her stomach, tightening even more as she slowly held out the card to the man. "Here it is."

By this time Reggie had joined Dani at her side. She put her arm on Dani's shoulder. She could hear the pain in her friend's voice.

The man could see Dani's hesitation in giving up the card. He waited patiently for her to hand it over. He carefully took the card, still in its plastic covering. He looked down through his reading glasses perched at the end of his nose. "Let's see what we have here," he sighed softly. A long pause. The man's eyebrows arched upwards as his interest in the card increased. "This is quite a specimen, young lady. You've taken very good care of this."

"Yes, thanks."

"Where did you get this? It's quite a rare card."

"It was my grandfather's. He gave it to me. Jackie Robinson was his favorite player."

"Well, he took fine care of it also. It's in excellent condition. Let's see what we can work out." The man, who Dani now assumed was the owner, walked to the end of the counter. He reached underneath and pulled out a *Beckett* magazine, the same issue Dani had just seen in the bookstore.

"Hey, isn't that the magazine we just saw?" piped in Reggie.

"Yeah, that's it," said Dani. "The low value on the card is $700," Dani added, just loud enough for the man to hear.

"Yep, that's true. $700," Reggie chirped. Now she felt she was helping.

"Well," the man chuckled, "it seems you girls have done your homework." He put the magazine back without looking any further, knowing that amount was probably right. "Here's what I can do," he said as he walked back toward the girls. "I've got to leave a little room for profit if I can sell it. So, I can offer you"…a long pause. Dani held her breath. "I can offer you $850 for it."

"Wow!" Reggie blurted with excitement. Dani, however, stood motionless. This was it. The moment of truth. If she said yes and took the money there was no going back. She stood there, thinking, remembering, feeling. Everything the card meant to her—everything Pop meant to her—flashed in quick scenes behind her eyes. The pause seemed like a lifetime, but it was only a moment, a moment that ended when Reggie spoke softly and caringly to her, slipping her arm around Dani's neck.

"Dani…what are you going to do, sweetie?"

With her eyes closed, she did it. She said it: "O.K., I'll do it."

"Are you sure," the man asked carefully. Dani nodded silently. "O.K., I'll be right back." He went into the back room of the store and returned a minute later with money in his hand. He counted the crisp bills out into Dani's hand…"six, seven, eight hundred, and fifty." The man looked up at Dani and smiled. All Dani could return was the slightest of grins, lips pinched tightly together. The man saw that she had a hard time selling the card. He was curious why she was doing it and wanted to ask, but he didn't.

Dani leaned over the counter to look at the card one last time. It now started to sink in that she would never see it again. The reality of this bit her like a snake, sharp and deep. Before the tears came again she turned away, stuffing the money into her pocket, mumbling a "thank you" to the man on her way out.

Chapter 17

Bobby strolled slowly down the hospital corridor, one hand thrust in his pants pockets while the other held a sandwich for his mother. He was heading back to Pop's room. He didn't want to leave his mom for too long. He felt she needed support right now.

As he entered the room Bobby saw his mother close to Pop's bed. Tears were rolling down her cheeks.

"Mom, what is it?"

"The doctor just left," she sighed. "He's a different doctor—a heart surgeon." Edith had a difficult time saying the last part.

"A surgeon," Bobby uttered. "What did he say?"

"Your father's heart has two passageways blocked. He's going to need surgery to fix them." Edith looked at her son with a sad, helpless expression. Bobby moved to her, hugging her with both arms.

The girls' bus ride home was pretty quiet, nothing more than boring small talk. Dani was deep in thought, confused with her emotions. She was glad she had enough money to go see Pop, but still devastated over giving up the card. Every few minutes she would slide her hand over the bulge in her jeans from the money in her pocket. She'd never had that much money before. However, the money didn't feel exciting or cool. It felt weird. It felt heavy, a burden she didn't want to have to carry.

"When do you think you'll leave?" Reggie asked, breaking one of the long silences.

"Well, I heard flying at night is cheaper. Maybe I'll do that."

"How much will it cost?"

Dani sighed. "I'm not sure. But, I think I have enough for a round-trip ticket."

The girls reached their stop and got off the bus. The silence returned as the girls walked briskly home. The many things that Dani had to do made her walk at a quicker pace than normal.

"Are you in a race?" asked Reggie kidding, trying to keep up.

"Sorry, Reg. There's just so many things on my mind, I guess I wasn't paying attention."

"It's O.K. I know this has been hard for you."

"Yeah, it has," Dani confessed. She turned to look at Reggie. "But you being here with me, it did help. I don't know if I could have done it alone. Thanks for going with me, Reg." Dani stopped walking and gave Reggie a hug, feeling like she was about to cry again.

"Hey, hey, don't get all mushy on me, girl," Reggie said, trying to lighten the mood. "You would've done the same for me." Dani pulled away and smiled. She didn't know what else to say. It was one of those moments when best friends didn't need to speak to communicate. They just knew. They walked the rest of the way home without a word.

Chapter 18

With so many things bouncing around in her mind, Dani sat on her bed and closed her eyes. She wanted to stop the bouncing thoughts, put everything in order, not forgetting anything. Dani was good at this. By nature, she was a well-organized, logical person. Her school work was neat and sorted by subject in her binder. Her clothes were always folded and put away, not left on her bed or piled on the floor. Her shoes were lined up in her closet like soldiers standing at attention. Pencils and paper clips lived in pencil and paper clip containers, not scattered across her desk. Dani's life was tidy, sorted, and organized. That's how she liked it.

Right now she wanted to put her thoughts in the same orderly manner. First, she would pack. Wait. For how many days? Well, clothes for at least three days seemed logical. She could wear them more than once if needed. Second, she would call her mom at work. She needed to explain the events of this afternoon and her plans to leave. Third, get to the airport and buy a ticket. Fourth, call dad. Maybe he's got some information. Whew, that's a lot to do. But Dani didn't have time to worry about how many things she had to do. She just needed to take care of them.

Pop's hospital room was quiet even though there were three people in the room. The only sounds were the constant soft humming and beeps of the machines hooked up to Pop and the occasional squeak from the blue vinyl hospital chairs when Edith or Bobby shifted uncomfortably in them. There really wasn't much to say. All they could do now was sit with their fears and wait; wait for the doctor to return; wait for Harold to wake up; wait for the surgery to happen; wait for Harold to recover, hopefully.

Edith and Bobby's feeling of helplessness added to their frustration, which added to the silence, hanging over them like a thickening fog.

Bobby made a final squishy squeak from his chair as he rose and walked to the window. He wasn't looking at anything in particular. There wasn't much of a view. His mind wasn't on what he saw. It was on his daughter. Now was the time. Instead of just sitting here and waiting, doing nothing, he would call her. He had to do something. Besides, he owed it to her.

Chapter 19

Dani was putting the last of her socks in her bag when the phone rang. The piercing sound in the quiet house surprised her. She sucked in a quick gasp of air and held her breath. Who was calling? Was it grandma? Dad? Reggie? Pop? Was it good news, or...or.... The second ring rattled through the stillness of the house and halted Dani's rambling mind. She rushed to the kitchen. In the middle of the third ring she picked up the receiver, eyes closed tightly from fear, uncertainty, and hope. A weak, scratchy "Hello" came out of her throat.

"Dani?"

"Dad?"

"Yeah, baby, it's me. How are you?"

"Well, to be honest, I'm a wreck. What's going on?"

Bobby took a long pause. He thought for a moment about protecting Dani's feelings by not telling her everything. Maybe just a few details but leaving out the surgery. But that would be taking the easy way out—again. No. He needed to be truthful and honest with Dani. She deserved that.

Bobby relayed all the details he knew to Dani. He described Pop's current condition, what the doctors had said, and his approaching surgery. Dani listened carefully and silently on the other end of the phone. She didn't interrupt but tried to take everything in. It was hard to hear it. For the first time Dani realized just how serious Pop's condition was. She now knew she wanted to get there as soon as possible.

"Dad, I'm coming out there," Dani confessed. Bobby was surprised; surprised at the news and surprised at how determined Dani sounded.

"But...but...how are you going to do that?" Bobby asked.

"Well, I've been a little busy the last day or so," stated Dani. Now it was her turn to tell her story. She explained how she felt after hearing about Pop. She described how she thought of the card, wrestling with herself over whether to sell it or not, and going to the mall and leaving with the money for the trip to New York. Bobby listened to the whole story. He felt sad for her having to go through all that, giving up something so important to her and all the emotions she must have felt. At the same time, he was also incredibly proud of his daughter for how mature and responsible she was. His little girl maybe wasn't so little any more.

"Wow," exclaimed Bobby, "it sounds like you've planned everything out." Even though he controlled the tone of his voice so it wouldn't show, Bobby's heart was breaking. "When do you plan on leaving?"

"If Pop is going to have surgery, I want to get there as soon as possible. So, I'm going to leave some time today. If I call you from the airport, would you come and pick me up?"

"Of course, baby," Bobby said. "JFK airport is closer to the hospital if you can fly into there. You probably remember that."

"Yeah, that was my plan."

Dani and her father talked a few more minutes about meaningless stuff before she said she had to finish getting ready to go.

"O.K., then. Guess I'll see you tomorrow morning," Bobby said.

"O.K. See ya. And Dad…thanks."

Bobby smiled to himself. "Sure thing, baby. I love you, little girl."

"I love you too, Daddy," squeaked Dani with puddles beginning to form in her eyes.

Chapter 20

I want to operate as soon as possible." The surgeon's voice was soft but direct as he talked to Edith a few feet from Harold's bed. He was still unconscious.

"When is this going to start?" Edith asked helplessly, her hands fiddling nervously with a balled up tissue.

"I would like to start within the hour. His condition is stable right now. I want to take advantage of that and complete the procedure. I'll be back just before we take him in." The doctor walked through the door leaving both the room and Edith feeling more empty. She stood looking at Harold, still rolling and pulling on the tissue. She looked so lost and helpless.

She moved to the chair next to the bed. She reached out and put her hand on top of Harold's. "I'm here for you, sweetheart," she said aloud, hoping Harold could sense she was there.

"You want to leave when?" screeched Patricia.

"Tonight, mom. I need to leave tonight." Dani explained Pop's condition to her mother just as her father did to her a few moments earlier. Dani tried to stay calm and clear, but it wasn't easy. Every time she thought or spoke of Pop, it was like reliving the same bad dream, over and over again. Dani also described how she got the money for the trip. Repeating that experience was also painful, like describing how you just lost your best friend.

Although Patricia was impressed with her daughter's maturity and responsibility, she was still not very comfortable with letting her go. "Dani, I don't know about this. It has all happened so fast. Besides, I have to work late tonight. How are you going to get to the airport?"

"I'll take the bus to the airport. I know how to do it. Please, Mom. I went to all the effort, figured out a way to pay for it myself. I even…even…sold my Jackie Robinson card."

Patricia heard the pain in her daughter's voice. It was true. She did accomplish all of those things on her own. She did make a huge sacrifice to go by selling the card.

"We had a deal, mom. Remember? You said if I took care of everything and raised the money I could go." That was true, too. Even though Patricia didn't think Dani could do it, she did. She accomplished her goal.

"You're right, Dani. I said that thinking you couldn't do it, but you proved me wrong." Patricia sighed heavily. "You can go." On the surface, she was nervous about Dani going alone. Deep down, however, she was proud of her daughter; proud of her maturity, her responsibility, and the sacrifices she made for the love of her grandfather. She was grateful for the daughter she had.

"Thanks, Mom. Don't worry. I'll be fine. Dad will pick me up at the airport in New York. I'll only be gone until the end of the week."

"Dani, be careful," Patricia pleaded, already missing her.

"I will, Mom."

"I hope your grandfather will be all right. I'll be thinking good thought for him."

"Thanks, Mom. Me too."

Pop was being wheeled down the corridor to the operating room. There, the surgeon would attempt to repair his heart so perhaps he wouldn't have another heart attack. Even with the operation, Pop still had a long way to go.

Chapter 21

D ani had a seat in the middle of the bus. Fortunately, it wasn't too crowded so she could put her bag on the seat next to her. The total ride would take about forty-five minutes with the one transfer she just made. This gave her a little time to think.

As cars and buildings whizzed by she thought about which airline ticket counter to try first, thinking of the ones that might fly to New York. She thought about how long she might have to wait for a flight and when she might arrive. She thought about what day to make her return flight. That was Dani, always thinking.

She also thought about seeing her father. It had been a while. It would be nice to see him and stay with him while in New York. She just wished it was happening for a different reason. Dani used to stay with him on some weekends when she and her mother still lived in New York. She let her mind wander to those times when she was younger, going out to dinner when she stayed with her father, helping him make pancakes in the morning, staying up late watching funny movies. Other than her parents' divorce, Dani couldn't remember having too many worries back then. Life was simple. Even though it wasn't that long ago, it seemed like a thousand years had come and gone.

Before she knew it the bus arrived at Los Angeles International Airport. Dani grabbed her bag and marched into the terminal. She knew exactly where to go, of course, planning her moves while riding the bus. She found a monitor displaying the departures from Los Angeles. She searched for flights to New York and found one. She noted the airline and searched for their ticket counter, finding it in just a couple of minutes.

After standing in line a while it was finally her turn. She walked up to the counter. "May I help you?" the ticket agent asked pleasantly.

"I would like to buy a round-trip ticket to New York, JFK Airport, please."

The agent smiled. She was amused at the polite and confident girl in front of her. "Well, let's see what we have." She typed rapidly on her computer. "I can get you on our 10:00 flight this evening. When did you want to return?"

"Sunday."

"O.K.," the agent replied. More typing. "I have a flight leaving JFK in the afternoon on Sunday."

"That's fine," Dani said. "Um...how much will it be?" More typing. Dani held her breath. It seemed like the agent was typing a novel. Please be less than $850 Dani thought to herself. Please. Please.

The agent finally finished putting in the information. "That comes to $788 dollars." Dani could breathe again.

"Yes! Uh...I mean...O.K." Dani reached into her purse for the money, feeling totally embarrassed. She had tried to act so cool until that last outburst. The agent smiled at this again, seeing what Dani was feeling. Dani didn't see this last smile, burying her head down in her purse as an escape, wishing she could crawl into it.

A few moments later Dani was on her way to the gate, round-trip ticket in hand. Whew! That was over. She had done it. She was on her way to see Pop.

For the first time, Harold's eyes fluttered open. Edith and Bobby saw this and edged closer to the bed. Harold was still groggy but tried to focus on the two figures looming over his bed. He managed to crack a thin, weak smile.

Edith and Bobby talked briefly to Harold. They knew he was tired, so they wanted to keep it short. Bobby mentioned to Harold that Dani was coming. Harold's eyes brightened noticeably at the news. "I can't wait to see her," he said with a crackly, scratchy voice and a larger smile. This gave him something to look forward to.

Edith talked to Harold a little longer about what happened to him. He asked a few questions, but Edith did most of the talking. A moment later the surgeon came in. "Mr. Rogers, you're awake. That's good. How are you feeling?" The doctor spoke to all three of them for a few minutes. He expressed to all that the surgery went well. He asked Harold a couple of questions while looking at the chart. He answered a few questions from Edith and Bobby before moving to the door. Bobby walked with him and out into the hall.

"Doctor, honestly, how does it look?" Bobby asked, not wanting his mother or father to hear, but wanting the truth.

"Well, there are no guarantees with his age and condition. He's stable now, but the recovery process is a long one. The next day or two will tell us a lot more. Unfortunately, all we can do now is wait to see if he improves."

Bobby didn't like the news, but it was what he expected. He nodded his understanding with a grim expression. "All right. Thank you, Doctor."

Chapter 22

The wait in the airport seemed to last forever. Dani tried to pass the time by reading some things for that she brought. It worked for a while, but she was fidgety and restless. She wanted to be on her way.

Finally, the nearly four hour wait that felt like two days was over. She had boarded the plane and was in her seat. She got lucky and had a window seat. She wouldn't have much to see since she was flying at night, but she liked sitting by the window anyway. No one would cross in front of her and that horrible food and beverage cart the flight attendants pushed couldn't smash into her leg. Having a window seat was just fine with her.

Before take-off Dani's mind wandered to Pop. It would often during the flight until she saw him. She wondered how he would look. She hadn't seen him in a few years. She expected being sick and in the hospital could change his appearance. In her imagination she planned for the worst but hoped for the best. This made her sad. She so wanted to walk into his room and see him just as she always remembered him. When she recalled all the wonderful times and precious memories with Pop, she pictured him like she always did—fun, full of energy, and loving. She didn't want him to be different. She wanted him just like he is in her dreams. She wanted nothing to change. Things, however, had changed. Baseball games in the sunshine, sitting on the couch watching TV, Pop handing her the Jackie Robinson card for the first time, these were the memories that drifted through Dani's mind. They kept her company for most of the flight. She held them close and guarded them now, like a prized possession. They had to replace the ones she had sold.

The plane landed in New York a little more than five hours after taking off, right on time. Dani walked down the ramp that connected the plane to the terminal. She felt tired, only dozing restlessly during the flight. However, she also felt excited. She had made it back to New York. Home. Where she started. Where so many good things from her life were. Where the people and memories made her who she was.

She was also very close to seeing Pop. Her joy at this almost made her weariness disappear. She quickened her pace as she walked through the almost deserted terminal. To Dani it felt like 3:30 in the morning. But in New York, three hours ahead of Los Angeles, it was 6:30. No wonder she felt tired and the airport was quiet.

She walked passed rows and rows of empty chairs, looking for a phone to call Dad. He had told her to call him on his cell phone when she arrived. Down the wide aisle running through the middle of the terminal Dani found a phone and her father's number from her pocket. After one ring Bobby answered.

"Dad, I'm here."

"Harold, Dani is on her way," Edith said softly, leaning close to Harold's face. "Bobby just left to pick her up."

"That's good. It gives me something to hang on for." Harold shifted in his bed wincing. He was tired, uncomfortable, and in pain.

"What do you mean 'hang on?'" Edith questioned. "You're going to be fine. You're a tough stubborn old goat." Edith smiled when she said this. It was not the first time she teased him by calling him an old goat. "Dani will be here soon. The doctors will take care of you, and you're going to be home before you know it." Edith was trying her best to reassure Harold and make him think positively. She was also trying to convince herself.

Chapter 23

Bobby's car cruised down Pennsylvania Avenue. Early morning work traffic was out, but it wasn't too bad. Bobby and Dani were catching up with each other about recent events in their lives. They talked about everything except for the reason Dani was there. Pop. They both seemed to know that those emotions would come out when they arrived at the hospital. They tried to avoid facing them as long as possible.

Bobby and Dani rode in silence for the last few minutes as they turned on Clarkson approaching the hospital. Dani had stalled as long as she could but could wait no longer. "Dad, how is Pop? Really. I want the truth."

Bobby sighed. He was waiting for Dani to ask. "Well, honey, he's weak. Your grandfather is getting older, and he did have major surgery. The doctor said the surgery went well. But, it's not over yet. He still had a long way to go. We don't know anything for sure." Bobby paused, thinking of what else to say. Dani sat silently. "He was glad to hear you were coming. It made him smile." Dani smiled at this too. It made her want to cry. She could feel the emotion swelling up inside her like lava rising in a volcano. She capped it, though. She wanted to keep her emotions in control. She wanted to be positive around Pop; crying may upset him. Also, if she started crying now it may be harder to stop once she was in to see him.

Dani and her father walked through the entrance of the hospital and toward the elevators. Bobby led the way and pushed the elevator button. A car came quickly and the doors slid open, inviting Dani and Bobby inside. Again Bobby worked the button. The elevator car lurched upward giving Dani's stomach that funny dropping feeling. She took a couple of deep breaths, trying to calm the variety of emotions whizzing through her. She felt nervous, scared, and excited all at once, each emotion competing for control.

The doors opened and Dani followed her father down the maze of hallways to the Intensive Care Unit. She approached Pop's room and peered in, stopping at the entrance. She saw machines with tubes and wires leading to the bed and into Pop. Bags of clear liquid hung above him. A tube ran into his nose to help him breathe. Pop looked older, weak, and fragile. The scene wasn't what Dani expected. Even though Dad had explained it, seeing it with her own eyes came as a shock. How could she expect her grandfather to look so tired and helpless when she held such beautiful images and memories of him? She hesitated before entering.

It was still Pop, however. When he looked up and met Dani's eyes nothing else mattered, not how he looked, not what she remembered. All that mattered was Dani and her grandfather were together again.

She rushed to his bedside. She clutched his hand with her right and wrapped her left arm around his neck. She gently kissed his cheek. "I've missed you so much," she whispered. With the little strength he had Pop hugged her back.

"I'm glad you're here, Dani," hissed Pop, sounding like he was talking on a phone full of static.

Dani left his side for a moment to see her grandmother, giving her a big, warm hug and kiss. They all talked for a moment, catching up a little, before Bobby jumped in. "I think we should give Dani some time alone with our patient. She did come a long way to see him."

"Of course," Edith added, "but Dani, maybe you should do most of the talking. Your grandfather is still too weak to hold long conversations. He would love to listen to you."

"Sure, Grandma. We've got a lot of time to make up for." She looked back to her grandfather and smiled.

"I want to hear everything," Pop wheezed, patting the bed to signal Dani to come to his side.

Edith and Bobby left the room. Dani dragged one of the squeaky blue chairs up to Pop's bed. She held Pop's hand again and began talking.

The longer she was there the better she felt. The excited emotion was defeating nervous and scared inside her. There was no competition any longer. It was like being back home. Being with Pop made things seem right. After a while she wasn't thinking much about him being sick. She was reunited with him, and that was all she cared about. It was like they were the only two people in the world.

Dani told Pop about school. She talked about her classes, her teachers, and her friends. She told him her last report card was straight A's. "That's my girl," Pop added softly, smiling proudly.

Dani then wanted to talk about the two of them. She wanted to reminisce about the times her and Pop had. She brought up experiences the two of them shared. She was able to recall details unforgettably burned into her memory.

"Remember when we used to go to the park? We'd play catch, and you would throw me pop-ups and grounders. And after that we'd go to the swings. You pushed me hard, but I kept saying, 'Higher, Pop, higher. I can fly!'" Dani laughed out loud. It had been a while. She hadn't laughed for days.

"Yes, I remember," Pop whispered. He had a pleasant, genuine smile. He was enjoying listening to these stories again and to the sound of Dani's voice.

"And remember when I would try pushing you on the swing? I was too little to push very hard, but you would say 'Higher, higher!'"

"Yeah," Pop said, barely louder than a breath.

Dani switched the conversation to baseball. Of course this would eventually come up. It was their bond, their tie, their link to each other. She recalled specific details of certain games they attended. Great catches, big home runs, important victories.

"Remember when we saw…and remember the time when…." Dani rattled off these events perfectly, as if they happened only yesterday.

As she continued she noticed Pop's eyes close. "Hey, Pop. We can talk later. I should let you rest."

"No, no," Pop pleaded with the little energy he had left. "Keep talking. I'm just going to close my eyes…I'm listening." He forced the last two words out with a heave and a sigh, a simple, peaceful smile softening his face.

Dani continued narrating the episodes of her and Pop's story. She talked about eating hot dogs at almost every game. She talked about the catcher she laughed at when Pop described his equipment to her. She had so many more memories to share when she stopped and asked: "Pop, what was your favorite game?" A pause. "Pop."

Suddenly, a machine in the room sprang to life. It was the one monitoring Pop's heart. His had stopped. The loud repetitive beeping pierced through the peacefulness of the room and through Dani's soul. Her eyes widened, panic creeping into the sound of her voice. *"Pop! Pop! Can you hear me? Answer me, Pop! Stay with me! Don't go! Don't go!"* She held his hand tightly and kissed his forehead. She leaned next to his ear and whispered: "I love you, Pop. Don't leave me. I just got to see you. Don't leave me, please."

At that moment, hospital staff entered the room. Dani pulled away so they could work but didn't want to leave his side. She backed away helplessly to a corner of the room. This couldn't be happening, she thought. Things were going so well. She was just talking to him.

The staff worked on Pop for several minutes, but his heart had simply stopped. They tried hard, but there was nothing they could do. He had peacefully slipped away while Dani spoke to him.

Pop was gone.

Dani stood in the corner until after the staff left. They gave Dani some privacy with Pop. She walked slowly to the bed and picked up his hand in hers. Tears rolled down Dani's cheeks and dropped on to the bed covers. She looked at Pop's face, no longer etched in pain and weariness. It almost looked like the faintest hint of a smile remained on his lips.

After a long cry, Dani wiped away her tears with the back of her hand and sighed deeply. She couldn't stop looking at Pop's face, how peaceful it seemed now.

She wondered if Pop left this world in just the way he wanted—talking about baseball and great memories with the person which he shared a special bond. From the look on his face, maybe he was just…ready. It was as if he had waited until Dani arrived to spend one last time with her.

She dragged the chair back to the side of the bed. She grasped Pop's hand again and picked up where she had left off. "What was your favorite game, Pop? Well, I think mine was the time when we saw the Mets and the Cubs. Remember that one? The Mets were down by two in the bottom of the ninth. The first batter…."

Chapter 24

Dani walked home from school alone. She had stayed after in the library, getting some books for her history project. She had been back three weeks. The schoolwork she had missed was all made up. Things were pretty much back to normal. That nagging empty hole in the pit of her stomach she had been carrying around since Pop died seemed to get a little smaller each day. Dani had a feeling it would never truly go away completely. She would always have Pop and his absence with her.

She reached her house and grabbed the mail before unlocking the front door. Once inside she tossed the mail on the kitchen table for mom like she did every day. She hung her backpack on the chair and headed to the refrigerator. She poured a glass of orange juice and headed to the living room to watch a little TV before starting her homework.

As she passed the table something looked odd. Dani glanced at the stack of mail. An envelope, larger than the others and cardboard, stuck out part way from underneath the ads and a magazine in the pile. It must be important, Dani thought. She pulled it out of the pile and stared at it. It was addressed to her. It was from her father.

She anxiously tore the tab across the back and opened it. She pulled out a letter:

Dear Dani,

I'm so sorry for all the pain you've gone through recently. I know how much you miss Pop. I miss him, too. I feel so bad for all the sacrifices you made to see Pop, only to get to spend a very short time with him. I decided the least I could do for my daughter was to try and ease your pain. I know I haven't always been there when you've needed me. So this time, I wanted to do the right thing. I don't have to remind you to take care of it. I know you will.

I love you, baby girl.

Dad

P.S. See, I do listen to you.

Dani read the letter a second time. It made her feel good that her father wrote to her. He was thinking about her. She smiled as she put the letter on the table. But she was also confused. What did Dad mean by taking good care of "it"? And what did he mean in the P.S. about listening? Dani paused for a moment wondering. She picked up the large envelope. It felt like there was still something inside. She tipped it over and a small rectangle covered in wrapping paper fell onto the table. She carefully peeled back the paper and gasped. It was the Jackie Robinson rookie card...*her* Jackie Robinson rookie card.

Dani held it in front of her and stared. She began to cry. She cried because she had the card back after having so much difficulty parting with it. She cried for the caring and thoughtfulness of her father. She cried for Pop.

After several minutes of staring at the card, emotions of all kinds washing over her, Dani wiped her eyes. She walked toward her room, a content smile on her face. She needed to call Reggie about this, but there was one thing she had to do first.

Dani flung open her closet doors. She reached inside, way down in the back behind her shoes. She grasped and pulled out the white box with the bright green ribbon. She placed it on her bed along with the card. Still smiling, Dani carefully untied the ribbon and opened her treasure chest. She picked up the plastic encased card and slipped it safely to the bottom of the box, back to its rightful resting place.

Dani understood that the card wasn't going into her treasure chest because it was her most prized possession. Pop was her greatest treasure. It just...belonged there.